This Ladybird Book belongs to:

_____

_____

_____

_____

This Ladybird retelling
by
Nicola Baxter

Acknowledgment
The publishers would like to thank John Dillow
for the cover illustration.

Published by Ladybird Books Ltd
80 Strand London WC2R 0RL
A Penguin Company

15 17 19 20 18 16

Printed in Italy

FAVOURITE TALES

Sleeping Beauty

illustrated
by
GAVIN ROWE

based on the story by Charles Perrault

Once upon a time there was a king and a queen who had long hoped for a child of their own. When, at last, a baby princess was born, they thought that a good fairy must have been looking after them.

"I shall invite all the fairies in the kingdom to come to our baby's christening!" cried the King joyfully.

When the time for the christening
came, the King was as good as his word.

Among the guests were the twelve good fairies who lived in that land. After the grand feast, each of them gave a magic gift to the baby girl.

"You shall have a lovely face," said the first.

"You shall be gentle and loving," said another.

One by one, they promised the little Princess all the good things in the world.

When eleven of the fairies had given
their gifts, a furious voice was heard
at the doorway.

"I suppose you thought I was too old to do magic now! Well, I'll show you!" it shrieked. And a very old fairy, whom everyone had forgotten, walked slowly towards the cradle.

"When the Princess is fifteen years old, she shall prick her finger on a spindle and fall down dead," she cursed, and rushed from the palace.

The King was horrified. "Oh, how can I have forgotten her?" he cried. "And what shall we do now?"

"I may be able to help," said a gentle voice.

It was the twelfth fairy. "I can't undo the evil spell," she said, "but I can soften it a little. The Princess will prick her finger on a spindle, but she will not die. She will just fall asleep for a hundred years."

The King and Queen were very
grateful to the twelfth fairy, but still
they did not want anything to happen
to their precious daughter. They
made sure that all the spindles in the
kingdom were destroyed.

Year by year, the Princess grew more lovely. Surely no one could want to harm such a kind and gentle girl?

On the morning of her fifteenth birthday, as the Princess wandered through the palace, she climbed to a high tower where she had never been before. There she saw a wooden door.

Pushing it open gently, she peeped inside. There sat an old, old woman at a spinning wheel.

"Good morning," said the Princess. "What are you doing?"

"I am spinning, my child," said the old woman. "Look!" and she handed the Princess the sharp spindle. At that moment, the Princess pricked her delicate finger!

At once, the Princess fell into a deep, deep sleep. The wicked fairy's words had come true.

At the same moment, everyone in the palace fell asleep as well.

In the great hall, the King and Queen
fell asleep on their golden thrones.

The lords and ladies, the palace
guards, and all the servants fell into a
deep slumber. The whole palace was
silent and still.

As the years passed, a hedge
of thorns and brambles grew
up around the palace walls.
It grew so tall and so thick that
at last only the flags above the
highest towers could be seen.

The story of the beautiful
sleeping Princess spread
through the kingdom and
far beyond.

She became known as the Sleeping Beauty.

Many princes came to the palace, hoping to rescue the Princess, but none could force his way through the thick, sharp thorns.

Almost a hundred years had passed
since the Princess had pricked her
finger, when a handsome young
Prince from a faraway kingdom
happened to pass by.

On the road he met an old man,
who remembered a story that his
grandfather had told him. And so it
was that the Prince heard the legend
of the Sleeping Beauty.

"I shall not rest until I have seen her
and woken her," he vowed.

When the Prince saw the great hedge
of thorns, he nearly despaired. But
when he raised his sword, the thorns
suddenly turned into lovely roses, and
the hedge opened to let him through.

Inside the palace gates, all was .
The dogs lay asleep in the courtya.
The guards slept at their posts. Even
the pigeons sat asleep on the
rooftops. Not a sound could be heard.

The Prince searched the entire castle.
He found the sleeping King and Queen
and their sleeping servants. But it was
not until he reached the very last
room in the highest tower that he
found Sleeping Beauty herself.

He gazed at her lovely face in wonder.
"I would give my whole kingdom if
you would wake and be my bride," he
whispered.

Then he bent over and gently kissed
the sleeping girl.

At the touch of the Prince's lips, Sleeping Beauty awoke. As she smiled at him, she felt as if she had loved him all her life.

Throughout the palace there were sounds of laughter. Everyone woke and rubbed their eyes. They could hardly believe that the evil spell had been lifted at last.

As for Sleeping Beauty and her Prince, they were married soon after. And the King made sure that *everyone* was invited to the wedding!